Pajama Light

BY Gale Sypher Jacob

ILLUSTRATED BY Mark Graham

Dutton Children's Books

Lighthouse time, sun sinks low.
Pajamas, sneakers, set to go.

Hand for Daddy, hand for Bear,
step out, sniff the sea-salt air.

Pajama walk again tonight.
Here I come, Pajama Light!

Down the driveway, pebbles crunch.
In clover patches, rabbits munch.

Through the woods, pine-needle ground,
I pillow-walk without a sound.

Down the hill, we stop halfway.
The Johnsons' dog wants to play.

We cross the field of bushes, stumps;
I climb gray rocks like whaleback humps.

On the path through sumac hedges,
off I race to seaside ledges.

Here I am, Pajama Light,
on the highest rock again tonight!

Windblown waves smack the shore.
Seagulls shriek, circle, soar.

Red-hot sun sinks away.
Fiery clouds fade to gray.

I count the boats as they go past,
waiting, waiting,

THERE! At last!

Flashing lighthouse gleams for me,
and for the ships far out at sea.

Hello again, Pajama Light;
watch me wave to you tonight.

In navy sky the spot of white,
blinking twice, says good night.

Daddy's shoulders are my chair.
Hand on Daddy, hand for Bear.

Pajama night-light, bedtime sky,
it's time to go, good-bye, good-bye.
On the path at end of day,
like boats, we turn the homeward way.

We cross the field, this time I'm tall,
the whale-hump rocks look flat and small.

Up the hill, a Daddy ride.
The Johnsons call their dog inside.

Through the woods, long pine boughs stir,
night wind whispers, whisper, whir-r.

Up the driveway, rabbits gone,
sleeping, hidden, until dawn.

Above tall fir trees, birds in flight
swoop to branches for the night.
Darkness hugs us, house ahead,

Daddy whispers, "Time for bed."

A hug, a kiss, then close my eyes.

The shushing sea sings lullabies.

To Chuck, Andy, Nona, Christopher, John, and Amy
—G.S.J.

To Shiraz and Zarene
—M.G.

DUTTON CHILDREN'S BOOKS
A division of Penguin Young Readers Group
Published by the Penguin Group

Penguin Group (USA) Inc., 375 Hudson Street, New York, New York 10014, U.S.A.
Penguin Group (Canada), 90 Eglinton Avenue East, Suite 700, Toronto, Ontario, Canada M4P 2Y3
(a division of Pearson Penguin Canada Inc.) · Penguin Books Ltd, 80 Strand, London WC2R 0RL,
England · Penguin Ireland, 25 St Stephen's Green, Dublin 2, Ireland (a division of Penguin Books Ltd)
Penguin Group (Australia), 250 Camberwell Road, Camberwell, Victoria 3124, Australia (a division of
Pearson Australia Group Pty Ltd) · Penguin Books India Pvt Ltd, 11 Community Centre, Panchsheel Park,
New Delhi 110 017, India · Penguin Group (NZ), Cnr Airborne and Rosedale Roads, Albany, Auckland
1310, New Zealand (a division of Pearson New Zealand Ltd) · Penguin Books (South Africa) (Pty) Ltd,
24 Sturdee Avenue, Rosebank, Johannesburg 2196, South Africa · Penguin Books Ltd, Registered Offices:
80 Strand, London WC2R 0RL, England

Published in the United States by Dutton Children's Books,
a division of Penguin Young Readers Group
345 Hudson Street, New York, New York 10014
www.penguin.com/youngreaders

Designed by Beth Herzog and Abby Kuperstock

Manufactured in China
First Edition

ISBN 0-525-47385-8
1 3 5 7 9 10 8 6 4 2